The Littlest
BIGGEST
Helper

Written and Illustrated by
Steven Lane Taylor

Enlightenment Lane

SEDONA, ARIZONA

The Littlest Biggest Helper
Text and Illustrations
Copyright © 2016
by Steven Lane Taylor

For more information, please contact
Enlightenment Lane, the Publishing Division of
Steven Lane Taylor, LLC
1020 Crown Ridge Road
Sedona, Arizona 86351
info@rowrowrow.com

ISBN-13: 978-0-692-73470-4

For
Cole and Tanner,
Simone and Philip,
Tristan and Taylor,
and . . .

Once upon a time, there was a very little elf. Which brings up a question you might be asking yourself. "Isn't *every* elf little— every single one?" Yes. But this was the *littlest* . . . second to none!

Elves, you see, grow up fast—
just not tall.
They reach their full height
in no time at all.

They get big enough, in fact,
to start working right away.
And they help
in Santa's workshop
each and every day.

But this elf grew slowly—
much slower than the others.
He was too small to work
with his sisters
and his brothers.

To see over a table
he had to stand on a stool.
And his hands were too tiny
to hold a single tool.

The little elf was sad,
because he wanted to
help out. After all, elves
are helpers—that's
what they're all about.

Then the elf realized
there was one thing he could do
to prove to Santa Claus
that he could help out too.

If he wasn't big enough
to help *make* the gifts and toys,
he would help *deliver* them
to all the girls and boys.
To get down a chimney he was
just the right size!
Santa needed
magic, or
several
tries.

So the night before Christmas,
as Santa prepared for his flight,
the elf asked Santa,
if he could help him
that night.

Santa said, "I'm sorry, no."
And he told the little elf,
"This is a trip I always take
by myself."

Well, the little elf heard
what Santa had to say.
But he was determined to go . . .
anyway!

Are you wondering right now
what the little elf did?
He got in Santa's sleigh
and behind some gifts . . .
he hid!

When at last the time had come
for Santa Claus to go,
he climbed into his sleigh
and chuckled,
"Ho, Ho, Ho!"

The reindeer started running
and they sailed into the sky.
They flew very, very fast
and very, very high.

13

Santa soon landed
at the very first house.
But the elf stayed hidden,
as quiet as a mouse.

When Santa slid down
the chimney
with his sack of toys,
the elf went right behind him,
without making noise.

The elf brought a present
with a big red bow. But
he stayed out of sight,
so Santa wouldn't
know.

While Santa wasn't looking,
he put his gift with all the rest.
He was a great little helper—
maybe the best!

Before Santa was finished,
the elf returned to the sleigh.
He hid himself again,
and they were soon up and away.

At the very next house, something
slipped Santa's mind.
Santa went down
the chimney,
but left his toy
sack behind.

Not knowing who lived there—a girl or a boy— the elf grabbed a gift that both could enjoy.

He dropped down the chimney, looked here and looked there, but he didn't see Santa Claus anywhere.

There were no decorations—
not even a tree.
And there were no signs
of children,
as far as he could see.

The little elf was puzzled.
What was going on?
Why had Santa stopped here?
And where had Santa gone?

Then the elf heard something—a sound up on the roof. It was Santa! He was leaving! He'd be gone in a poof!

The elf raced up the chimney, but he was too slow.
Santa was already gone.
Oh no! Oh no!

The little elf was left behind, cold and shivering. And worst of all, Santa Claus didn't know a thing!

The elf went back into the house
and curled up in a chair.
And that is where
they found him—the couple
who lived there.

They got up in the morning
and could not believe their eyes.
An elf was sleeping in their chair!
What a big surprise!

The elf woke up and explained things to the woman and the man. Then they all sat down together and came up with a plan.

The elf would stay right there until the following Christmas Eve. That's when Santa should return, and then the elf could leave.

That meant the elf would live there for one entire year, which brought the couple so much joy, they almost shed a tear.

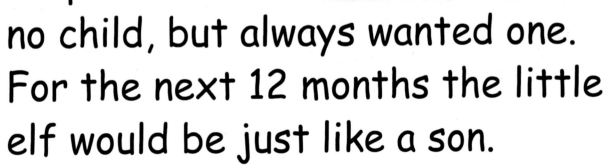

You see, this couple had no child, but always wanted one. For the next 12 months the little elf would be just like a son.

And so in January,
in cold and snowy weather,
the couple and the little elf
began their year together.

The three of them
went sledding down a steep
and slippery hill.
They almost all fell out!
It was quite a thrill!

They built a great big snowman
and threw snowballs
at each other.

They drank hot chocolate by
the fire—one cup, then another.

In the spring they flew some kites and picked a bunch of flowers.

They had a picnic in the park and tossed a ball for hours.

When warmer weather came, they went swimming in a lake.

They always stopped for ice cream and a great big chocolate shake.

In the fall they jumped in leaves that were raked up into piles.

They went for walks on country roads for miles and miles and miles.

Finally December came, and Christmas Eve was near. It wouldn't be too long before Santa Claus was here.

They started decorating and putting up some lights. The excited little elf began counting down the nights.

The elf would soon be leaving,
which made the couple sad.
They had grown
to love him.
They would miss
the little lad.

And then the night arrived
that they'd been waiting for.
All three of them were wishing
they could have a few days more.

They sat around the fireplace,
eating cookies baked that day,
and listened very closely
for the sound of Santa's sleigh.

At twelve o'clock that night they heard a jingle overhead. Then down the chimney Santa came, in his suit of red.

"Santa!" cried the little elf,
"I've been waiting here for you!
I bet you wondered where I was.
Did you even have a clue?"

"I hid myself in your sleigh last year," the elf went on to say. "I was left here accidentally when you flew away."

Santa Claus began to smile, and then let out a chuckle. And finally he laughed so hard he almost popped his buckle!

The couple and the little elf  were a bit confused. Why was Santa laughing? Why was he amused?

Said Santa to the little elf, "Before I have to go, there is something I must tell you. There is something you don't know. When you were very, very young—maybe three or four—I found you sleeping on the steps outside my workshop door."

"I don't know where you came
from, or why you are so small.
Your ears aren't even pointy—
not like an elf's at all.

But like an elf, you want to
help. You really, really do.
And I believe that I have
found the perfect job
for you."

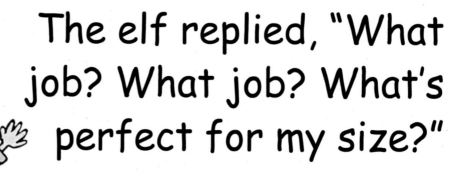

The elf replied, "What job? What job? What's perfect for my size?"

And that's when Santa Claus revealed another big surprise: "Last Christmas Eve, I saw you when you sneaked onto my sleigh. I knew you were behind me the whole, entire way!"

49

"This man and woman  need a child—not a game or toy. I brought you here so you could be their precious little boy."

And that is how the little elf
came to understand: He was
here on purpose.
It was something
Santa planned!

"I might be little,"
thought the elf,
"but Santa is so clever,
he found a way for me to be
the biggest helper ever!"

52

Then Santa asked the little elf,
"So what's it going to be?
Would you like to stay
with them, or will you leave
with me?"

The elf knew in an instant—
he didn't want to go!
He loved the couple very much.
And oh, they loved him so.

They had fun together from
the moment that they met.
It didn't matter if the day
was windy, cold, or wet.

The elf knew he
belonged *right here*,
not in the frozen north.
He wanted *this* to be
his home, from
this day going forth.

Santa's
Workshop

So the elf said to the couple,
"I want to live with you."
Which made them both so happy,
it was like a dream come true.

Santa said, "I wish you well,
but now I have to fly."
Then up the chimney Santa went,
before they blinked an eye.

They ran outside and waved goodbye, as Santa disappered. They loved that jolly man with his bushy, snow-white beard. For he had given all of them a present like no other . . .

59

It was the gift to be a family—
a father, son, and mother.

Made in the USA
San Bernardino, CA
08 September 2016